# Spot's First Walk

## Eric Hill

PUFFIN BOOKS

# Off you go, Spot!

# Don't get lost.

# Not in there, Spot.

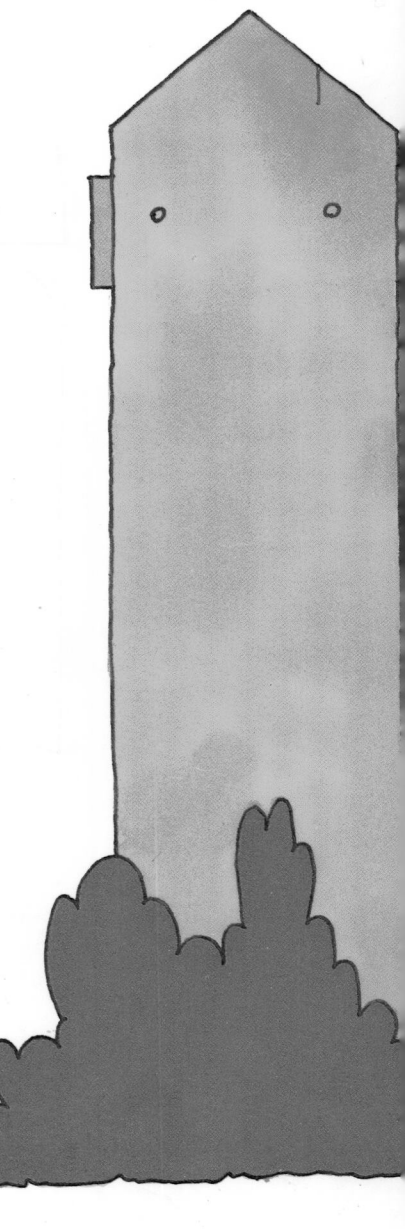

# Watch out!

# What's in the coop, Spot?

*tap* ... *tap* ... *tap* ...

*tap* ... *tap* ... *tap* ...

# That's a funny noise ...

... and that's
a nice smell.

# What have you found?

# Now for a drink ..

# Poor Spot! Time to go home.

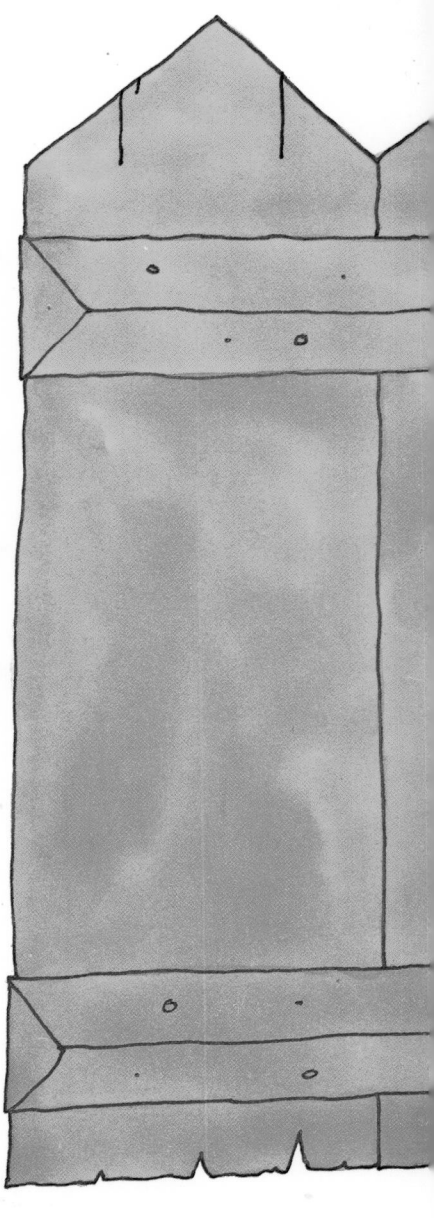

# What <u>have</u> you been doing, Spot?

Nothing.

PUFFIN BOOKS
Published by Penguin Group
Penguin Young Readers Group,
345 Hudson Street, New York, New York 10014, U.S.A.
Penguin Books Ltd, 80 Strand, London WC2R ORL, England
Penguin Books Australia Ltd, 250 Camberwell Road, Camberwell, Victoria 3124, Australia
Penguin Books Canada Ltd, 10 Alcorn Avenue, Toronto, Ontario, Canada M4V 3B2
Penguin Books (N.Z.) Ltd, 182-190 Wairau Road, Auckland 10, New Zealand

puffinbooks.com

First published by G.P. Putnam's Sons, 1981
First paperback edition published in Great Britain in Picture Puffins, 1994
Published in the United States of America by Puffin Books, 1994
This colorized edition published by Puffin Books,
a division of Penguin Young Readers Group, 2004

007 - 10 9 8 7

Printed in Malaysia

ISBN 13: 978–0–14240–085–2